W9-CFE-281

DISNEY's

DOUG™

Created by
Jim Jinkins

CHRONICLES

Itchy Situation

by Jeffrey Nodelman

Illustrated by Vinh Truong & Tony Curanaj

Itchy Situation is hand-illustrated by the same
Grade A Quality Jumbo artists who bring you
Disney's Doug, the television series.

DISNEY
PRESS

New York

Original characters for "The Funnies" developed by Jim Jinkins and
Joe Aaron.

Copyright © 1999 by Disney Enterprises, Inc.

All rights reserved. No part of this book may be reproduced or transmitted
in any form or by any means, electronic or mechanical, including photocopy-
ing, recording, or by any information storage and retrieval system, without
written permission from the publisher. For information address Disney
Press, 114 Fifth Avenue, New York, New York 10011-5690.

Printed in Mexico.

1 3 5 7 9 10 8 6 4 2

The artwork for this book is prepared using watercolor.

The text for this book is set in 18-point New Century Schoolbook.

Library of Congress Catalog Card Number: 98-87733

ISBN: 0-7868-4299-7

For more Disney Press fun, visit www.DisneyBooks.com

Disney's

DOUG™

Created by
Jim Jinkins

CHRONICLES

Itchy
Situation

CHAPTER ONE

Doug and Porkchop sat in the living room watching television, when a commercial came on for the newest Race Canyon movie, *Race Canyon 16: Quest for the Sock of Gold.* It opened in Bluffington Friday night, and Doug couldn't wait. The whole gang—Doug, Patti, Skeeter, Beebe, Connie, Chalky, and

Roger—always went together to the first show of a Race Canyon movie. Everyone was up for it, especially Doug. He hoped that this time he'd get to sit next to Patti at the show!

Doug imagined that this would be like one of those fancy-shmancy Hollywood movie openings. The press would be there, with photographers and television cameras, as all the movie stars stepped out of their limos to walk down a long red carpet to the front door.

Cameras flashed in Doug's mind as hundreds of screaming fans (who couldn't get tickets) stood

behind ropes trying to get auto-
graphs. Then a brand-new limo
pulled up. The whole crowd
watched breathlessly, waiting for
the door to open. When it did,
Doug Funnie, dressed in a white
tuxedo, stepped into the spotlight.
Girls screamed out his name and
held up signs that read WE LOVE
YOU, DOUG!!! He politely waved
and turned to help his date out of
the car. It was the lovely Miss
Patti Mayonnaise. She was
dressed in an elegant evening
gown by Fraud DeSigner. She
took Doug's hand as he escorted
her down the red carpeting.

Race Canyon said, "Hi, Doug, so

glad you could make it! Here, let me get the door."

"Thanks," Doug said. "Let's do lunch soon." Then he and Patti walked inside the theater.

When Doug felt Porkchop pulling at his pant leg, he

realized he had been daydreaming again, but now he was hogging the popcorn. He couldn't wait to go to the premiere. It would be perfect.

CHAPTER TWO

The next day Doug and Skeeter walked home from school together, talking about the premiere. It was very exciting.

"So who do you think will show up?" Skeeter asked. "Do you really think Race Canyon will be there?"

"I don't know," Doug answered. "I read that he was already filming *Race Canyon 17: The Other Sock.*"

As they reached his house, Skeeter asked, "You want to come in and kill some mutant space weeds?"

"Sure," Doug said. "This time I know I'll get a high score on Mutant Weed Killer 2000!"

Downstairs in Skeeter's room, they were so involved with the game that they didn't notice they weren't alone. "Get that one!" Doug yelled. "No . . . the variegated one! Look out for the Creeper . . . over there!" The television was making tons of noises, blips, and beeps, and loudly exploding vegetation shook the room. Skeeter worked the joystick like a pro, maneuvering his space lawn mower into position to mow the oncoming poison ivy into space mulch. Doug yelled again, "Right behind you!" Just then Skeeter's little brother, Dale, jumped into Doug's lap!

"AAAGGHH!!!" Doug and Skeeter yelled. Skeeter dropped the joystick and Doug instinctively grabbed Dale. "Where did you come from?" Doug asked.

"Juice," Dale said with a grin.

"Where?" Doug asked again, a little confused.

"Juice!" Dale replied with more force.

Skeeter said, "He wants some juice. Man, you're gonna have to learn baby lingo before Dirtbike starts to talk, honk honk."

"Well then, juice it is," Doug said, as he gave Dale a piggyback ride upstairs into the kitchen.

Doug got the sippy cup while

Skeeter got the juice. That's when
Doug noticed the notes all over
the kitchen. They said DON'T

FORGET and FRIDAY NIGHT and REALLY IMPORTANT.

"Wow," Doug said. "You must be really excited about the premiere on Friday if you left this many notes for yourself."

"I am," Skeeter replied. "But they're there to remind me that I have to baby-sit for Dale on Friday night. It's my dad's tugboat reunion, and they're going out for dinner with his old crew."

"Wait a minute," Doug said. "How are you going to go to the movie if you have to baby-sit?"

"Wow, man," Skeeter said. "When you put it like that, I guess it's impossible, honk honk."

13

"Can't you find someone else to baby-sit?" Doug asked. "It's Race Canyon!"

"My mom tried," Skeeter explained. "No one wants the job because he's got the . . . " He whispered, "P-O-U-L-E-T P-O-U-L-T-R-Y P-O-X. As soon as he starts to itch, he's gonna get real cranky."

Doug spelled out the letters in his head and then looked at Dale in his arms. With frightened eyes, he looked back to Skeeter and gasped, "POULET POULTRY POX?"

"Shhhh!" Skeeter said quickly. "He doesn't know yet. It takes a couple of days to show up."

Doug quickly put Dale down. "Aren't they really contagious?" he asked.

Skeeter replied, "Only if you never had them. Some kid in Dale's day-care class has them, so now the whole class is infected."

"I gotta go," Doug said, hurrying to the door.

"Where are you going?" Skeeter called after him. "You can only get it once, and everybody gets it when they are babies."

Doug didn't answer. He was already gone.

CHAPTER THREE

Outside, Doug crashed into Roger and his gang. They were on their way to the Four-Leaf Clover Mall when they heard Skeeter yelling, and then Doug bounced right off of Roger. "Sorry, Roger," Doug said. "I guess I wasn't watching where I was going."

"No kidding, Funnie. What's your big hurry, anyway? Your little pal

Skeeter have the cooties?" Roger said, dusting himself off.

"Uh . . . no, I just forgot . . . that I, um . . . have to go . . . home," Doug said nervously.

By this time, Skeeter had caught up to Doug and said, "Hey man, why'd you run off like that? Just because Dale has Poulet Poultry Pox doesn't mean that you'll get them. It's like a baby disease. Everybody in town had it when we were in kindergarten."

As soon as Skeeter stopped talking, he realized that Doug hadn't gone to kindergarten in Bluffington. He had moved here when he was nearly eleven.

But before he could say anything, Roger cut in. "What's the matter, Funnie? Don't tell me that a baby like you never had the Poulet Poultry Pox! What's the matter? Are you . . . CHICKEN?" Willy, Boomer, and Ned burst out laughing.

"No!" Doug said. "Of course I had the Poulet Poultry Pox . . . I think. I had it when I was a baby, just like everybody else. I gotta go now. Call you later, Skeet." And Doug hurried home.

Roger yelled after him, "Aw, come on now, Funnie, I didn't RUFFLE YOUR FEATHERS, did I?" His gang rolled with laughter.

Roger looked at Skeeter and said, "You don't think I'm being too FOWL, do you?"

Skeeter just ignored Roger and turned back into his house. He had not only exposed his best friend to the Poulet Poultry Pox, but he had also embarrassed him in front of Roger. He felt terrible.

CHAPTER FOUR

The whole way home, Doug tried to remember when and if he had ever really had the Poulet Poultry Pox. Since only babies got it, maybe he had been too young to remember. He still had a chance.

As he walked, Jumbo Street started to turn into a jungle. Light posts turned into huge trees, and the wires became long vines. Exotic-looking flower bushes sprang up out of nowhere, and Doug's house transformed into an ancient stone temple. Doug was no longer Doug, he was Race Canyon!

Race was in the fight of his life. The Voodoo Poultry People were hunting him! The tribe chased him all through the jungle. He had to swing from trees and jump across great rivers just to keep away from them. If they caught him, their evil spell would cause the worst case of Itchiosis ever known to man! Race had eluded them for twelve long years, and

he wasn't about to give up now.
He kept running.

At last, he came to a small
clearing. He looked around. There
was no sign of them.

He breathed a sigh of relief.
Just then, a giant chicken of a
man popped out of the bushes.
And then another one, and
another, until Race was
completely surrounded by Voodoo
Poultry People! They started to
close in on him. Race pleaded,
"Aw, come on, you guys. Can't we
talk about this?"

Suddenly, he had an idea. He
looked up at the sky, pointed, and
said, "Look! Is that a flying

chicken?" As all the Voodoo
Poultry People looked up, Race
ran in the other direction. He was
safe, but for how long?

CHAPTER FIVE

When Doug got home, he found
his mom in the kitchen with
Dirtbike. "Mom," he said, avoiding
the baby, "what would happen if,
say, for instance, someone got
exposed to someone else who had
Poulet Poultry Pox?"

"Well, Douglas, it *is* very contagious. If someone comes into con-
tact with the disease, he should

start to look out for little pink dots. And itching, of course. Why do you ask, dear?"

"Oh, well, it's nothing, really. Just wondering. Skeeter says Dale's got it. But I don't need to worry, anyway, since I had it as a baby, right?" Doug said anxiously.

"No, dear. So you should probably stay away from Skeeter's house for a week or two. Okay, son?" his mother answered.

"Sure, Mom. I'll do that," he replied sadly.

Upstairs, Doug lay on his bed feeling sorry for himself, with Porkchop right beside him, equally depressed. How could this have happened?

All he could think about was Skeeter saying, "Only babies get the poultry pox." Doug knew Skeeter hadn't meant anything bad by it, but how could he get a

baby disease? He imagined himself at school the next day. The hallways were filled with students and when he walked out of class, he was wearing nothing but a diaper! Everybody pointed and said stuff like, "Look at the little baby, isn't he cute?" Even Patti asked, "Would the sweet little baby like his bottle now?" Doug groaned.

He sat up in bed. He had better call Patti now and tell her what had happened. This was so embarrassing. He called Patti and started to tell her the whole story, but before Doug had a chance to tell her that he might be infected, too, she interrupted him.

"Oh, no," she sighed. "That's terrible. I hope Dale feels better
soon. But with Skeeter out,
unless you're about to bail, too, it

looks like it's just me and you for the movie."

"What?" Doug was confused. "What happened to everyone else?"

"Well," Patti replied, "first Beebe called to cancel. She has to go with her dad to the ribbon-cutting ceremony of the new Beebe Bluff Mall. Then Chalky found out his basketball team has a play-off game that night. Connie's new band is playing at the intermission, so she can't go. Even Roger has an excuse. His limo's in the shop, and he's not coming unless he can make a big entrance. So with Skeeter out, I guess it's just you and me. You're not going to let me down, too, are you, Doug?"

"Of course not," Doug said, squirming. "Why would I let you down? I'll pick you up, unless the theater burns down, or an asteroid hits the earth or something. It's not like I have Poulet Poultry Pox or anything."

"Sure, Doug," Patti said, a little confused. "Well, see ya."

As he hung up the phone, Doug knew he had just told Patti a lie. He was just too embarrassed to tell her the truth. How could he tell her that a grown man of twelve years might have a baby disease? What if she laughed?

What if she thought he didn't
want to go alone with her?
Why did his arm itch all of a

sudden? As he scratched, he decided that he was going to beat this. No baby disease was going to keep Doug Funnie down!

CHAPTER SIX

The next day at school, Skeeter met Doug at his locker to apologize.

"I'm sorry, man," he said. "I guess I just wasn't thinking. We've been best friends for so long now, I don't remember what it was like when you weren't around. So I just assumed that you got the Poulet Poultry Pox when I did."

"It's okay, Skeet," Doug answered. "It's not your fault. Besides, I'm not a hundred percent sure that I really have it yet anyway. Some people could be so strong that they're immune to it."

"Then why are you scratching your neck?" Skeeter asked.

Doug didn't even realize he was doing it. "Oh, it's nothing," he said as they headed down the hall to the lunchroom.

Just then, Roger and his gang showed up.

"Hey Funnie," Roger said. "What's scratching?"

"Very funny," Doug said, getting in the lunch line. "Nothing is scratching with me, how about you?"

"I'm all grown-up, Funnie," Roger answered. "Only a baby like you could get a baby disease now!" Laughing, he and his gang went to pick up their trays.

Behind Skeeter, Larry, one of the A.V. nerds, spoke up. "I heard

your little brother has the Poulet Poultry Pox and you're looking for a baby-sitter," he said. "Well, look no further, I had it when I was three, and I'm not busy Friday night."

I had them when I was three, Doug thought. What a show-off!

"Wow," Skeeter said. "That's really nice of you, but my mom thinks it would be better if I stayed home with Dale. He's starting to break out big-time, and boy, is he ever cranky!"

"Yeah, I remember how bad those spots were," Larry said. "First they start off small, just a few dots here and there, but then they spread, and spread, and spread—all over your body, and scratching doesn't help. It just makes them itch even more. And then just when you think it can't get any worse . . . "

"Hey!" Doug interrupted. "Doesn't the mystery meat look delicious today?"

Just then Patti, Beebe, and Connie joined them in line.

"Hey, guys," Patti said. "How's it going?"

"Perfect," Doug answered quickly. "I'm perfect, we're perfect, everybody is perfect."

"That's good, Doug," Connie said. Then turning to Skeeter, she asked, "How's that adorable little brother of yours?"

"Oh, he'll be just fine in a couple of days, once he stops scratching," Skeeter replied.

"It's a good thing everybody gets the Poulet Poultry Pox when they're little," Beebe said. "If you got them when you were bigger, you'd have even more of them."

"Yeah, imagine that," Doug said, fidgeting. "A big kid getting the poultry pox, how ridiculous can you get?"

"Yeah, how ridiculous." Patti laughed uncomfortably. Then she tried to change the subject. "Hey, how about that Race Canyon

movie? We're still on, aren't we,
Doug?" she asked, hiding behind
Beebe as she scratched her arm.

Doug thought for a moment.

Here was his chance to get out of the mess he had gotten himself into. All he had to do was come clean and tell Patti the truth. But he had gone too far to turn back now. Besides, everyone was looking at him. Now just wasn't the time. He answered Patti, "Of course I'm okay. I'm in perfect health. There's nothing to stop us from going to the premiere."

"Great," Patti said. "It'll be great." But she didn't seem excited.

Doug thought, Patti doesn't seem very excited. Maybe she knows I have Poulet Poultry Pox. But I can't let her down! I won't!

CHAPTER SEVEN

That day after school, Doug told his mom he was just itching to get started on a project in his room. As soon as he shut the door, he dropped his books and started to scratch like wild. Porkchop just shook his head as if to say, "Poor guy."

"Man, Porkchop, this is awful," Doug complained. "I don't have

any dots yet, but I can't stop
scratching. Remember when I got
poison ivy on that Bluffscout
camping trip?"

Porkchop nodded as he began to
help Doug scratch.

"Well, compared to this," Doug
continued, "that was nothing!" He
sat down to write in his journal,
while Porkchop picked up a news-
paper to read.

Dear Journal,

Man, who'd have thought so much trouble could start just by playing with Dale! Now I itch like crazy, and I just don't know how to get out of this mess! I wish I'd told Patti I never had Poulet Poultry Pox from the very beginning. Then I'd feel bad about missing the movie with Patti, but not because I lied to her, too!

As he put his pen down, Doug looked at his best nonhuman friend and said, "What am I gonna do, man?"

CHAPTER EIGHT

The next morning, when Doug woke up, for a minute he didn't itch. "Yes!" he said out loud. "I beat it! I knew I could beat it! No baby bug can keep me down! I *can* go to the premiere!" Then he noticed Porkchop was staring at him with his jaw wide open.

"What is it?" Doug asked.

Porkchop continued to stare, pointing to the mirror.

Steadying himself, Doug walked over to the mirror. He took a quick peek. He was covered from head to toe in little pink dots. It was official. He had the Poulet Poultry Pox.

He went downstairs to breakfast to show everyone. His family noticed right away.

"Oh, my goodness, Douglas," Mom said. "You are covered in Poulet Poultry Pox! Now, you march yourself right back upstairs and get back into bed. I'll call the doctor."

Doug sighed. "I'll just call

Skeeter first and ask him to bring my homework." He picked up the phone and dialed. "Hi, Skeet," he said. "Well, I have the Poulet Poultry Pox. Can you bring my books and homework to me after school today? And if anyone asks where I am, especially Patti, just run the other way. Okay?"

"Oh, she won't ask, Doug. She just called to tell me that she's not coming today, either," Skeeter said.

"How come?" Doug asked.

"Well . . ." Skeeter said. "She probably doesn't want me to tell you that she has the Poulet Poultry Pox, so I won't. You're just going to have to call her yourself and find out."

"She has the what? Oh, no! Thanks, Skeet," Doug said as he hung up the phone. He felt terrible. Not only had he lied to the girl of his dreams, but he had probably infected her with Poulet Poultry Pox, too. But why didn't

she want him to know she had it?
She must really be mad at him!
He had better call her and face
the music. He had put it off too
long already.

CHAPTER NINE

Dialing Patti's phone number, Doug tried to think of what to say. "How do you apologize to someone for lying to them *and* for giving them a contagious disease?" he asked Porkchop. "Especially if that someone is Patti Mayonnaise!" Doug had never been more nervous in his whole life.

"Hello," Patti answered the phone.

"Uh, hey, Patti, it's me, D-D-Doug," he stuttered. "I, um, just got off the phone with Skeeter, and, well, I—"

"Oh, no!" she exclaimed. "He told you?!"

"Well, sort of," he explained quickly. "See, I called him to tell him I have the Poulet Poultry Pox—"

"You, too? I'm so sorry, Doug," Patti interrupted. "I didn't think you could get it twice. Oh, now you won't be able to go to the movie tonight, either! And I bet you got it from me!" she moaned.

"No, Patti, just let me tell you this," Doug said. He knew he had to get it over with once and for all. "I got it from Dale. And it's my first time. I lied to you. I'm so sorry. I guess I was embarrassed because Roger made it seem like I'd be such a baby to get it now and then things just got out of control, and I ended up giving it to you. I'm really sorry," Doug said, all in one breath. "Are you okay?" he asked.

"I'm fine," she said. "Just a little itchy, that's all. And don't worry," she continued, "you didn't give it to me. My dad did. He got it from someone at the gym where he goes to exercise. I was afraid to tell you because you made such a big deal about everybody having it as kids. I guess I was a little embarrassed, too."

They both laughed.

Then Patti said, "Maybe, since we're both sick, you could come over to watch a movie or something?"

"Sure," Doug said. "We could have our own screening of the first fifteen Race Canyon movies. I'll bring the videos and popcorn."

"And I'll have the back scratch-ers ready!" Patti laughed.

As Doug hung up the phone, scratching, he thought how great it was to have a friend like Patti. He still itched like crazy, but somehow, he felt good anyway. Funny, he had lied because he wanted to go with Patti to the premiere. But now he *was* going to sit next to her at the movies— all fifteen of them—because he had told the truth! Funny how these things work out!